Rose with No Thorns

Rose with No Thorns

ISBN: 979-8-9883457-3-2

Editor: Crystal S. Wright

10 9 8 7 6 5 4 3 2 1

Printed in the United States

Priceless Publishing®
pricelesspublishing.co

love can hurt...

Contents

But it can also heal...

Who is Karrington Rose?

As Karrington Rose looks around her room, she realizes that her summer at home is coming to an end. She is preparing for college at Alabama A&M University, the same HBCU where her parents met many moons ago and also her brother's alma mater. It will not only be far from home, but she anticipates a little culture shock as well.

Morgantown, West Virginia is all Karrington has known for 18 years being one of two black girls at Morgantown High School wasn't easy. Moving from home to what seems like the other side of the world, Alabama, she has no idea what to expect. For the first time in her life, she will be around people who look like her, and the mere thought was intimidating her. Karrington knows how to navigate social situations and try to "fit in," but this time the environment was people who look like her. Coming from West Virgina, this new experience was both exhilarating and scary for her.

As she continues to go over her packing checklist, Karrington gets ready for her going away party.

Her mom appeared at her door, looked around, and said to Karrington, *"Baby, are you almost done packing your tubs?"*

Karrington took a big sigh and replied, *"Mommy, do you think I'm going to fit in? Do you think I'm moving too far away from you and Daddy?"*

Her mother smiled. *"Baby, you need this. Your dad and I met in college and going to A&M was the best decision our parents let us make. Now, I'm not saying I won't miss you, but you need to do this for your future."* Her mother walked into the messy room, leaned over, and kissed her daughter's forehead. She reminds Karrington that she only has two weeks before she leaves. Karrington falls back on the bed and looked around the room. It was time to get back to work.

As her mother reached the door, she turned and said, *"Kelsey is still here and she is enough for me to stay busy and miss you at the same time. You will be great, baby. You need to figure it out and 9 hours away is not bad. You will thank me later. Now, get back to packing. You and Gabby's party is tomorrow and you won't want to deal with this after the party."* With that, she left the room.

Karrington's mother, Katherine, has always pushed her children while spoiling them at the same time. *Karrington needs this cultural change, so though it's going to hurt to see her leave, I know it's important that I let her go.* Morgantown was a challenging hometown for all of her children. Neither Katherine nor her husband had wanted their children to face any adversity, but it came with the Morgantown territory. Karrington is quite reserved and is the first girl to leave home. As Katherine walks away from her daughter's room, she looks back and prayerfully whispers, *"Lord, watch over my baby."*

Katherine spent the better part of the day bossing her husband, Fletcher around to ensure the party was well planned. Currently, she was worried their daughter's surprise gift would not be ready in time. *"Fletch, there is still no car in the garage and did they make the bow that I asked for!"*

Fletcher Rose is a man of leisure who generally does what he wants, except when it comes to Katherine Rose. For her, there is nothing he won't do. *"Katie, they will bring the SUV when it's time, baby, with the bow you picked out. I got this,"* he assures her. As she turns to walk away, he taps her behind and says, *"We have only one more to go and you know what that means."*

Katherine turned around and said, *"Fletch, just remind me later after our guests have left and the kids are situated."* She kissed his lips to show her satisfaction with him getting his task done.

Katherine shifted her focus to the rest of the evening. The doorbell rang, it was Gabrielle and her mom. Gabrielle Wiggins and Karrington have been best friends since kindergarten. They learned to lean on each other because they were the only brown girls in attendance for most of their time in school. *"Gabby and Claire get in here so we can get this celebration started. We have some young women to celebrate!"*

Katherine had transformed the backyard into a pink garden with pink peonies, Karrington's favorite flower, everywhere. The table setting was fit for a wedding reception. Roses and peonies were positioned in the middle of long tables with gold-trimmed plate settings. In the background, the DJ played 90's R&B music as more guests began to arrive. The atmosphere felt comfortable.

Friends and family gathered to celebrate the ladies. The hours rolled by as everyone shared stories of their time in college and conveyed good wishes to the girls.

Fletcher looks over to Katherine and says, *"Everyone, let's go outside and see Karrington's surprise."*

Once everyone was gathered and heading to the front door, a man pulls up in Karrington's new car. Karrington burst into tears as her guests cheer. She is so excited! She runs and hugs her mom and dad.

"Thank you, mom and dad. I love you!"

Kelsey wraps her arms around her big sister and kiss her cheek. *"You made it easy for me. I can't wait to get my new car when I graduate!"*

Midnight had come and gone and guests gradually leaving. The party was a success and now it hits Karrington for real that she will be leaving to start a new chapter.

Gabby spent the night so she and Karrington could go over their checklist for college. *"Karri girl, we will be on our own next week, are you ready?"*
Karrington smiled. *"After tonight I think I am. Are you?"*
Gabby nodded happily.

They continued to chat until they fell asleep.

Karrington and her dad took turns on the 9-hour drive to Huntsville, Alabama, while Katherine slept. Karrington always loved spending time with her dad. They talked and kept each other up on the drive. She loved listening to his stories about college and how he and her mom had met. Finally, Karrington had a chance to fall asleep.

She lost track of time but began to wake up when she felt the car slow down. As she wakes up, she sees that they are approaching the Alabama A&M campus.

Fletcher looked over at her and realized she knew exactly where she was. He saw the concern on her face and said, *"Pudding, you are going to be alright. All you have to do is call if you need anything! I have touched bases with the dealership here so if you have any problems with your car, you can take it in. Lastly, don't let anyone break your heart."*

Karrington knew that this was a conversation her father had waited to have with her. Though he is a military man, Karrington can feel his love for her when he calls her "Pudding."

Fletcher gets a little quiet as Katherine wakes up and starts to give directions from the backseat. *"Fletch, you could have turned in up there. Where are you going?"* Fletcher never says a word. He had intentionally taken the long way to delay the inevitable. Karrington turned to address her mother and got a glimpse of her dad's face as a tear rolls down his cheek.

Karrington could see this was hard for him. She put her hand on his arm and said quietly, *"Thank you, Daddy."*

As they drove up the hill to Thigpen Hall where Karrington and Gabby would share a room, they noticed all the other female freshmen who were moving in. There must have been close to 200 girls going back and forth between vehicles and the Hall, not including their loved ones.

Karrington and her family unloaded her luggage while they waited on Gabby and her mom to arrive. Having done this, they still had some time to drive Karrington around campus and show her some of her class locations. Once Gabby and her mother arrived, Karrington and her parents helped to move her things in. Everyone pitched in to decorate the room that the girls would share. When they were finished, the girls were satisfied with their little home away from home.

Gabby and Karrington went out to eat with their families before saying their goodbyes. After they returned to campus, it hit them like a ton of bricks — this was the first night of the next chapter of their lives.

Gabby sits on her bed and says with a nervous laugh, *"Karri girl, we are on our own. What do we do now?"*
"Girl, let's go see what the block is about."

With that, they decided to go out and see the campus. The girls exited their dorm and were immediately culture shocked! Never before had they been around so many black people who look like them. In West Virginia, they were in the minority but on this campus, African Americans outnumbered other races. The girls kept walking down the block and were fascinated by all that they saw. They saw the members of sororities and fraternities hanging out at a restaurant and the student center.

This excited both of them. Although Gabby was generally the most outgoing of the two, Karrington was beginning to feel different. She felt she could be a new person in college and possibly discover something new about herself.

"Gabby, I'm going to enjoy this. I can't wait for the party tonight!" Karrington and Gabby went back to their rooms to look for outfits for the party.

Karrington was excited about the "Welcome Freshmen" party being held at Dancing Room Only. When she and Gabby made it back, their new suite mates had arrived and were settling in. *"Hello! Are you our new roomies?"* Gabby asked in a bubbly tone.

"Oh hello, yes. I'm Lillian Walker and this is Morgan St. James. We just met."

 The ladies introduced themselves and shared what they had discovered on their mini tour of the block. They also informed Lillian and Morgan about the Welcoming Freshmen party. Lillian and Morgan were excited and excused themselves to finish their unpacking. The four of them planned to go to the party together.

Gabby exited the bathroom and started to gather her makeup items. Karrington, who had opted to use the bathroom mirror to get ready, immediately gathered her things and went into the bathroom. Karrington wrapped her reddish brown hair into a bun and started her face regimen. As she washed her face her skin you could tell her skin was like silk.

When she returned to the room, Gabby had finished her makeup and was taking rods out of her hair. Gabby had black, flowing hair that looked like a sheet of satin as it fell on her mocha-colored shoulders. Her hazel eyes made it hard for one to not stare at her. Gabby was truly a beautiful girl inside and out. She always seemed to have it together, even in Morgantown where the odds were stacked against her. Karrington always admired her 'take no shit' attitude.

Gabby had laid a nude backless dress out that was a little low cut in the front. This could be a lot for the first time out as a freshman. Gabby reached for the dress and broke into Karrington's thoughts. *"Girl, I hope this dress isn't too much for tonight. But why not right?"*

The girls laughed and continued to talk and dress. As Gabby let her dress fall over her head and the way it hit every curve, she was ready.

"Gabby, you look amazing! Let me hurry up," Karrington complimented her friend as she wiggled into her simple black dress. Hers was more conservative and hugged her body without being skin-tight. It was just low-cut enough for her comfort level. A couple of minutes more and the girls were ready. They went to check on their new suitemates.

The four girls made it to the club and it was everything they'd expected. There were fraternity guys, sorority girls, athletes, and people who have been out of college forever with 401Ks. They got on the dance floor and danced all night. They met some new people, some of whom would impact their lives for the next four years. This was a night of new beginnings for the girls. Karrington, Gabby, Lillian, and Morgan had only just met but on this day a lifelong bond began.

The girls got back to their suite and stayed up late to recap their night. They didn't fall asleep until morning. College life had just begun.

Growing Up...

As college life continued and forced them to grow up, the four ladies remained together. Gabby and Morgan were nursing majors, Karrington majored in criminal justice, and Lillian in theatre. In their sophomore year, they pledged sororities. Karrington, Lillian, and Morgan pledged AKA and Gabby pledged Delta. All the while they stay focused on their studies and had a great college experience.

The ladies visited each other's families on weekends and some holidays, and always had each other's back. The fall semester of their junior year would prove to be the biggest trial they would ever face. It would make or break their bond.

Gabby decided to attend summer school to take an extra course, while the other three girls left campus for the summer. She knew most of the students in her class, but there was a guy who she had only seen once or twice before. Randall Adams a biology major who was working on becoming a doctor. She remembered him from a class they had taken before.

Gabby and Randall decided to work on a project together. The time they spent together allowed them to get to know each other better and one day he asked her out. Randell was very smart and he was different from the guys who usually tried to talk to Gabby, so she accepted. They spent a lot of time working on their project and their relationship. Gabby was very happy. Even though her girls were not present, she kept them up to date on every detail. One night Gabby called Morgan, who she'd become really close with. She still had a strong bond with Karrington, but she spent most of her time with Morgan because they were both nursing majors. Gabby and Morgan had a lot in common.

"Mo!" Gabby squealed with excitement as Morgan answered the phone. *"So, I met a guy and I think I like him."* Gabby paused while Morgan silently listened. *"I think tonight is going to be the night!"*

Morgan was a little taken aback because it was unlike Gabby to like anyone who liked her. She was very careful about who she let into her space. Morgan was the most levelheaded one in the group. All three of the girls typically went to her before they made any decisions.

Morgan replied, *"You are down there all by yourself. Do you need me to fly down and talk you through this?"*
"No, girl. I got this. I will let you know how the night goes. When I get back, I'll call you," Gabby promised.

They talked a little more Gabby was sure to give her all of Randall's information before they hung up.

"Alright girl. Be careful and protect yourself. I love you," Morgan said.

"I love you too and I will talk to you later."

The girls hung up and Gabby started getting ready for the night.

Randall parked on the side of Terry Hall, the summer school female dorm, and ran in to pick Gabby up before SWAT could catch him. Gabby was ready and coming down the stairs as he walked in. She was wearing a red strapless dress and red heels. Her legs were the first place that his eyes went. As he walked up towards her, he could see her satin-like locks on her shoulders.

Her face lit up when she saw him. She sweetly said, *"Hello, Randall. I'm ready."*

Randall couldn't help himself. He had reached out and swept her into his arms and kissed her before without any conscious thought. *"Gabby, I'm sorry but I just had to kiss you,"* he said softly in his baritone voice.

Gabby didn't put up a fight. She kissed him back. *"Are you going to carry me out, Randall, or can I walk?"* That made him chuckle and kiss her cheek. He finally put her down and they walked to the car.

Randall had planned a great date. They went to the matinee, then to lunch period. After that, they went to a carnival in a nearby town. After that, it was getting late and he asked Gabby if she wanted to come over to his place. She agreed.

Once they got to Randall's place off campus, they were both surprisingly comfortable with each other. They talked about classes and what they wanted to do after graduation. Soon, they started to kiss. Randall was gentle and patient. He allowed Gabby to lead and this made her feel at ease.

Randall is tall and has an athletic build, this is what attracted Gabby to him from the beginning. He has a slender build as is typical for runners. His abs play hide and seek as he walks closer to Gabby.

He reached for her and placed her on top of him in one swift, fluid motion. As Gabby settled on his lap, her 5'2" frame seemed to magically shrink. She straddled him and they were face to face, breathing only each other's air.

Randall kissed her slowly, as his hands traveled down her frame and settled at the end of her dress. He lifted her dress and she felt her body reacting to his every touch. Then he lifts her again as if she was only a bag of feathers and placed her slowly on his erectness. Their gazes testified of their pleasure. Gabby and Randall continue to please each other for what seemed like forever until they reached satisfaction. Their night continued until the next day. They woke up side by side and explored each other's bodies all over again. Afterward, Randall took her back to campus.

Once Gabby got back in her room, she called her girls to give them the synopsis of her evening and morning with Randall. Karrington drilled her, knowing how careful her friend typically is with her heart. *"How long have you been seeing this guy? Why have I not heard of him before? What is really going on?"*

Gabby understood Karrington's concern and tried to ease her mind. *"Karri, I got this. I'm not too far gone. You don't have anything to worry about. Besides, I will see you and the other girls soon. Summer school will be over in two weeks. I can't wait to have a break!"*

Karrington hung up the phone and called the other girls. The only person that answered the phone was Morgan. *"Morgan, I just talked to Gabby and she is in summer school all by herself and in a relationship! I'm a little worried,"* she continued.

Morgan is the one who makes sure everyone is "OK" and she calms Karrington down. *"Karrie, she is going to be OK. You are going to be OK and we will all see each other soon. I've spoken to Gabby and she seems to be pretty happy with Randall. I just can't wait to see you all."* The girls continued to talk for a little while. They finally hung up and went to bed.

Gabby and Randall were inseparable for the next two weeks. They spent every moment together. They were taking the same classes and Gabby practically moved in for the remainder of her time in school. At the end of the session, Randall helped her pack her dorm room and accompanied her home so she wouldn't have to go back to West Virginia alone.

A trip that should have taken 8 hours took two days. They stopped in Knoxville, TN at Ruby Falls for much of one day to enjoy the waterfalls. The next day they stopped at Roanoke to go to the Harrison Museum of African Americans. They enjoyed their excursions together. Randall took her to Morgantown before heading to his hometown in Chicago. Gabby was excited to get home and introduce Randall to her parents and her best friend. She was anticipating Karrington's concerns.

As they got closer to Morgantown, Gabby told him about her parents and the friends that she wanted him to meet. He spoke about his family and suggested she comes up to meet his family too before the Fall semester starts.

Gabby was very happy. She reclined her seat to reflect for the next hour of the ride home. She felt good about Randall and had extremely high hopes for their relationship.

As students prepared to head back to A&M, Karrington and Gabby trailed each other back to school. Lillian prepared to drive in from Atlanta. The ladies planned to meet at the airport to pick up Morgan who was flying in from California.

The ladies were on their way to campus with Morgan, when she suggested that they stop at Pieology, their favorite pizza place. On the way to the restaurant, the girls wanted to talk about each other's summer but it was Gabby's that they wanted to hear about most.

They arrived at Pieology and took note of how each one had changed. Karrington's hair had been cut into a bob. Morgan seemed to have slimmed down and added highlights to her chocolate brown hair. Lillian finally got the braces she wanted and was visibly more confident. Gabby's style was completely different. She was covering up more than she used to. On this particular day, she was wearing jogging pants and a t-shirt instead of her usual shorts and a tank top. The summer changed the women a lot.

After they placed their orders, Gabby began to talk. *"I went to Chicago to see Randall and I think he may be the one!"*

The girls looked at each other in silence. Karrington had the most questions and eventually spoke up. *"So, Gabby, let me get this straight. You, who does not like anyone, have found the one. That's what you're telling me?"*

Gabby nodded and replied, *"I can change."* They laughed and continued to enjoy themselves before they headed back to campus.

Karrington's junior year was off to a good start. She was surprisingly acing the classes she needed and because she is an overachiever, she set a light schedule that would allow her to focus on her education after graduation. The schedule gave her a chance, for the first time to have three whole days without classes. On this particular Wednesday, she got up early anyways and went to breakfast.

Karrington walked into the cafe, she could hear loud laughter and she looked over to see members of the track and field team. No one was ever up before them.
When she got in line, she heard someone behind her say, *"Excuse me, are you new here?"*

When Karrington turned around to see who this deep voice belonged to and was coming from. There stood a tall, chocolate, man with dreads neatly pulled back and a smile that demanded her full attention.

"Hi. I don't usually get up this early, but you guys are up early every morning," she said.
"Well, I'm glad you woke up early today, Miss Sunshine. You have made my day. My name is Jonathan, Jonathan Thomas. What's your name, beautiful?"

Karrington smiled, moved up in line, and replied, *"Hi Jonathan. I'm Karrington."*

After that introduction, they were only apart for classes and track training. Jonathan was captain of the track team and an education major. He and Karrington have a great connection. They made time for each other but also learned the importance of respecting each other's passions and priorities.

Jonathan was not only the captain of the track team, but the team was actually at his mercy. He had won all six track events each season since his freshman year. He was the SWAC champion every year and put Alabama A&M in the elite division of track and field among HBCUs.

Jonathan had a strenuous schedule. He trained 4 hours a day most days, for a total of 20 hours per week. He was in talks with his coach about the prospect of being scouted to become an Olympian, which was his ultimate goal. He was so grateful for Karrington. She was the type of girl he was looking for.

Life in Morgantown had allowed Karrington to witness the treatment that her brother and father dealt with. She wanted to be an advocate for those who felt they didn't have a voice or no one in their corner. Like Jonathan, Karrington had a tough schedule. She was an excellent organizer who was able to have time for school, friends, Jonathan, and herself. It was so simple with them. There is an understanding between them that allowed them to respect each other's time whether they were together or apart.

***

Karrington was getting ready to go over to Jonathan's when she heard her phone ring. It was Lillian. *"Hey, girl. What's going on?"* Karrington asked.

Lillian was quiet at first. She finally said, *"Karri, we need you to come over. Now!"*

Karrington didn't ask Lillian a single question. *"OK, I'm on my way."*

They had moved into the same complex with one pair living across from the other. Lillian and Karrington surprisingly lived together while Gabby and Morgan roomed together. Karrington grabbed her keys and ran across the hall.

When she opened the door, she saw her forever best friend on the couch in a fetal position. Karrington dropped to her knees next to Gabby. *"What happened, Gabby? What's wrong?"*
Gabby slowly lifted her head. Karrington looked around the room at Morgan and Lillian's faces, then she looked back at her friend with tears in her eyes. The need for urgency had become clear. Gabby's eye was bloodshot and she had a cut on her bottom lip.

"What the fuck happened!" Karrington said angrily, crying through her words. *"Did Randall do this? Where is he!"*
Gabby had not yet offered an explanation as she was waiting until Karrington arrived. Gabby carefully tried to sit up as Morgan helped her to get comfortable. *"Randall and I were doing well. Y'all know that. We've been spending what I thought was a lot of time together. I got a call from some girl who said she was pregnant by Randall and she was his woman."*

The girls were in amazement. For the past semester, Gabby had been a little absent as she now spent most of her time with Randall. This was very confusing to all four of them.

Gabby continued. *"I called him because I just knew this had to be a joke, but how would someone I don't know get my number? When he answered, I said, 'Hey babe. What are you doing?' I always say something like that but for some reason, he got so aggravated with me when I asked that. I told him about the phone call that I had gotten and that I wanted to talk to him. I really wasn't worried about the girl at all, 'cause it's Randall. When would he have had time to do that? When he got here, we started talking about it. According to our conversation, the girl had gone through his phone which is how she got my number. At that moment I became worried and I had something to tell him."*

Gabby got quiet for a moment as the three girls continued to listen. *"I found out I am pregnant."*

The girls looked at each other bewildered. Lillian sat on the couch next to Gabby. *"Gabby, what did Randall do?"*

Gabby looked up and could read all of the hurt on her friends' faces. She felt safe and she began to speak. *"He told me that I was trying to trap him because I knew he would be a successful doctor. He said I was tricking him which was selfish of me."* She paused to take a deep breath. *"He knocked me down to the floor and told me how he hated what I was making him do to me. He kicked me in my stomach over and over and told me he never wanted to see me again. Then he left. I got up after a while and went to urgent care to find out I have lost the baby. I guess that's the blessing of all of this. What kind of father would he have been and what kind of mother would I have been in that environment?"*

Up until the moment when Gabby received a call from that stranger who claimed she was pregnant by Randall, Gabby had had no reason to believe Randall would ever cheat on her, much less hurt her physically. The girls surrounded her and held her as she wept.

Karrington got up from the couch and called Jonathan to tell him she would not be coming over because her friend had an emergency. Jonathan, understanding the relationship that she had with her friends, told her to call him if he could help in any way. She asked if he has bail money. They laughed and he told her he'll be home if she needs him.

Karrington hung up the phone and turned to her friends to figure out what she could do to make her feel better and put this political science education to work. She gathered as much information as she could without making Gabby more upset and told the girls that she would be right back. Karrington told Gabby she was going to her apartment to work on something.

Gabby knew there was no stopping Karrington. She looked up at her long-time best friend with swollen, teary eyes. *"Thank you."*

When Karrington got into her apartment, she broke down. Her heart broke for her friend that she's had all of her childhood. Now she's hurt differently than she's ever been hurt before. Karrington called a professor she trusted and explained the situation. They discussed it and came up with a solution. By nightfall Randall had been arrested, the school had been notified, and his parents were aware.

This made Karrington know that she had what it takes to be a great lawyer. Since Gabby didn't want to mention this to her family, Karrington and the other girls had no problem keeping her secret. She called Jonathan and told him she was going to spend the night with her friends. He told her that he loved her and said good night.

Gabby managed to continue to do well in her classes despite enduring such a traumatic experience. She didn't have to worry about running into Randall on campus. Once the school was notified of his actions with details from Gabby's hospital visit and witnesses, he was expelled immediately.

The girls continued moving forward. Gabby and Morgan started their nursing practicums. Lillian started her psychology practicum and Karrington continued to focus on her courses as she was entering her last year of classes. The ladies could hardly wait for the Christmas break.

The campus welcomed returning students and everyone was getting back into the groove of school. The ladies were settling well into the end of junior year. Back from the winter break, Karrington was hoping with the new semester and new season everything would be lighter. As for the other girls, they were preparing to bring in new pledges for their sorority. It's that time of the year when the weather is changing, and people go missing and everyone you haven't seen in three months pop up on the block completely affiliated with a Greek organization.

Gabby was doing great. She confided in her parents over the break. They took her to get counseling and set her up with a clinician at school so she could continue with her sessions. She was bouncing back. In fact, she was preparing to take over a line in her Delta Delta chapter. She is focused on finishing up her last set of courses, but tonight Miss Delta Sigma Theta was focused on her girls. Gabby addressed Morgan who was relaxing on the couch. *"Are you coming on the yard tonight?"*

Morgan was just getting in from dinner and her relationship with Gabby had grown in depth. Morgan was

sort of a protector. *"Girl, yes. I know you're excited and I expect to see you tomorrow night when my pretty girls show up and show out on the block!"*
They both laughed and got dressed. Morgan jumped in the car with Gabby and called the other girls to let them know that they were leaving.

While Lillian, Morgan, and Karrington waited on Gabby to complete her duties, they converse about their friend. *"Do you think she is OK?"* Lillian asked Karrington.

She turned to her Soror and said, *"She's getting there. I know sometimes she's bothered but she's really working. All we can do is be there for her."*

As the girls walked down from the AKA Stone, Gabby saw them and they meet up and get ready to leave. *"Girl, I'm getting too old for this stuff but I love it."* They laughed and headed to their cars to go home.

Karrington pulls Gab to the side and whispered, *"Girl, how are you really doing? You know that we are here for you and you know I am always going to be here."*

Gabby's eyes began to tear up and Karrington stood there as if she was ready to catch her. Gabby says, *"I'm OK. I'm taking it day by day. I love y'all."* With tears welling in her eyes, she continued, *"I thank you for everything. Thank you, Karri. Thank you for being my rock."*

Karrington grabbed her friend and hugged her tightly. *"Let's go, girl! We're all we got!"* The girls got in their cars and went to their apartments to get some rest.

As the semester began to wrap up, the students worked a little harder to finish strong. Karrington and Jonathan had inadvertently become the blueprint of how to navigate college while being in a relationship. Both of them were as busy as they were in love. Karrington was a bit upset that she hadn't seen Jonathan in a couple of days and it seemed like he was putting her off. Her phone rang and it was him. Suddenly, excitement bubbled in her belly.

"Hello, Jonathan!"

Jonathan re-positioned the phone and replied, *"Pretty girl!"*

When he calls her 'pretty girl' it usually brings a smile to her face, but today it was only a smirk. *"Jonathan, are you not busy today? When will I see you cause clearly, it's up to you."* Karrington was a creature of routine and when it's thrown off, so is she.

"Baby, I'm here. I sent you those texts for a good reason. Can we go out tonight?" he asked with hope in his voice.

Karrington answered, *"Yes, we can. I haven't seen the girls in a minute, anyway. Guess they have plans so I guess you'll do,"* she answered playfully.

Jonathan let out a sigh of relief and he told her he would pick her up at 8:00 and they hung up.

When Karrington opened the door, Jonathan was standing there with a lovely bouquet of roses. As soon as he saw her, his face lit up, and that smile that she loved so much appeared. *"You ready, baby?"* Jonathan asked.
Even though she wanted to be angry with him, she couldn't. Her joy at seeing him outweighed her little tantrum. *"Yes, baby. I'm ready."*

He opened the door of the car, helped her in, and kissed her on the forehead before closing the door. As they pulled up to the restaurant, Karrington was both impressed and concerned. How was he able to afford dinner at such a place?

As they walked into a large, private room of the restaurant, Karrington noticed that Jonathan's family was there. She turned to him, perplexed.

Jonathan smiled and filled her in. *"Baby, we are celebrating tonight. I know I've been missing for a couple of days but now I can tell you why. I was selected for the Olympics track and field team!"*

Karrington was overjoyed. She wrapped her arms around him and kissed him in full view of his family. She didn't care. She was so happy for him.

"I could not have done this without you!" he said as he held her close.

Jonathan made a speech to everyone in attendance who was celebrating this milestone with him. He disclosed how hard he has been working and how hard Karrington works. He publicly confessed that he truly loves and appreciates her for her unwavering support, even with her heavy workload.

As they were about to sit down to eat, Karrington heard the unmistakable voice of the first man who stole her heart.

"Pudding!"

No one else calls her that but her daddy. When she turned around and saw her father, mother, sister, and all her friends, she was both happy and confused.

"Daddy, what are you all doing here?" Karrington was happy to see her loved ones but she was still confused. As she embraced her sister and her mom, she repeated her

question. *"Guys! Will somebody please tell me what's going on?"*

Karrington heard the room grow quiet and turned around, curious. Suddenly, she understood. Jonathan was down on one knee! In an instant, her eyes began to fill with tears.

He opened a red, velvet ring box to reveal a lovely 1-carat, princess-cut diamond ring. As he looked up at his pretty girl with earnest eyes. *"Karrington, I want you for the rest of my life. Will you marry me?"*

Karrington looked back at her parents. As expected, Katherine was in tears and Fletcher was trying to hold his back.

Karrington looked back at Jonathan and answered him, *"YES! YES! I will marry you!"*

What an amazing night! Jonathan had gotten the best news that he has been chosen for the Olympics team and the woman of his dreams had made him the happiest man in the world. For Jonathan and Karrington, life was a dream.

Oh, what a great celebration it was. Karrington now knew why Jonathan had been so absent and she gave him her forgiveness over and over. As the night came to an end, she kissed her parents good night and they planned to meet for breakfast.

Jonathan took her home and walked her to the door. He knows Karrington, and this is why they make such a great couple. *"I know the girls are waiting on you." Smiling he added, "Now you know why they weren't around either."* When she opened the door, just as Jonathan said, the girls were inside waiting on her. Karrington kisses Jonathan and tells him how much she loves him.

He replied with a declaration of his love and admiration for her. He walked away smiling, as he heard the girls screaming with glee.

Senior Year...

Senior year went by extremely fast. Karrington was planning a wedding and focusing on graduation. Jonathan was finishing up his classes and working on his sponsorship qualifications and requirements for the Olympics. He would be graduating in the fall and moving to Colorado Springs to begin training.

Karrington had been accepted by DePaul University School of Law, as well as the University of Denver Sturm College of Law. Even though DePaul was her first choice, she applied to Denver Sturm since it would put her in the same state as Jonathan. Acknowledging that Jonathan was about to be her husband, she felt the need to compromise for the first time in a relationship. Deep down she knew she would not be able to go to DePaul because being with her husband is her first order of business. Being with her man and supporting him makes her happy.

Gabby would be graduating with Jonathan in the Fall. The summer she met Randall, caused her to advance in her classes and she was accepted at West Virginia University. She made the decision to move closer to home to get her Master's in nursing. WVU also happened to have practicum sessions in Morgantown. Even though it was not stated, Gabby was better. She wanted to be the best nurse she could be, so moving home would help her to both focus on her studies and heal.

Karrington, Lillian, and Morgan were all graduating in May. Lillian will be going to Columbia University in New York to do a Master's program and Morgan got accepted to West Virginia University too, so she will be with Gabby. Morgan could have gone anywhere, but the nurturer in her gave her no other choice. It worked out well because she would stay with Gabby and save money.

Everyone was excited about graduating, grad school, but what everyone was most excited about was the wedding. Karrington was over the moon and in complete bride mode as she prepared to marry her best friend. She was ready to start her life as Mrs. Jonathan Noah Thomas.

Becoming

MRS. JONATHAN THOMAS...

Graduation happened over a month ago and Karrington and her mother were putting the final touches on the wedding. Jonathan's mother was scheduled to come up from Missouri soon to help as well. To say Karrington was stressed right now would be an understatement. She was over her mom and this wedding. She was ready for all of it to be over.

"Karrington, why did you pick black and light blue for a wedding? Your bridesmaids are wearing black," Katherine said, making a face. *"Baby, why couldn't it be a little lighter or a little more summer?"*

Karrington needed a moment but her mother was in rare form.

"It's July 4th, I guess since you have blue," her mother continued.

Karrington took a deep breath and said, *"Mommy, this is my wedding. These are our favorite colors and Tiffany blue is not a regular blue. Put some respect on the color.*

Silver is in there and that lightens it up plenty." She went on to say that the event would be over in one day and the colors won't even matter.

Karrington was indeed happy to be marrying Jonathan, but she does feel like she's missing out on one thing — going to DePaul University for law school. Though she was content with the law school in Denver, it simply was not her preference. Compromising was new to Karrington, as was making decisions that would not give her a favorable outcome. But she learned in counseling that comprise is a part of marriage, she loved Jonathan so much she was able to be comfortable with her decision.

That's what marriage and becoming one are all about, right? As she drove to the airport, she had a rare moment to herself to reflect a little. *Girl, what are you doing? Why right now? He can go to Colorado and do his training and tryouts for four to five years and you can go to DePaul and do your three years.* Karrington continued to go over multiple scenarios in her head as she pulled up to the arrivals terminal to get her soon-to-be mother-in-law. *Might as well put it out of my mind because tomorrow is the big day.*

Karrington and her family had returned home from the rehearsal dinner. It hit her all of a sudden — this was her last day as Karrington Rose. Tomorrow she would be Mrs. Jonathan Noah Thomas and the weight of that was taking taking her breath away.

Kelsey appeared at her bedroom door and dashed for her big sister's bed. *"Hey, girl. How are you feeling? I love my dress, by the way."*

As Karrington stared at her sister, she realized how much Kelsey had grown in her time away. Kelsey was definitely not a little girl anymore. In fact, she will be starting at Bowie State University in the Fall. Karrington smiled and put her arm across her sister's shoulders as she explained her demeanor.

"Baby girl, I don't know how to feel. I love Jonathan and I want to be his wife. But I feel like I'm losing me," Karrington said with confusion in her voice.

Kelsey moved closer to her and said, *"You've always made the right decisions. If you want to run, I'll run with you. We can go to Fiji, right?"*

Karrington laughed as she hugged her sister. She told Kelsey that she was going to work on her vows.

The wedding day has come and it was a beautiful one. Karrington wanted to get married at home in her family's garden. This was one of her favorite places to talk and drink coffee with her mom. Katherine took so much pride in her green thumb and she had almost turned the backyard into a botanical garden that accepted paying patrons. The guests began to arrive. The music was now playing. Karrington is getting married!

Jonathan was in the dressing room with Karson, his frat brother, and Karrington's father. He was visibly nervous as he adjusts his Tiffany blue tie. A nervous talker, he felt the need to strike up a conversation. *"I really love Karrington. I'm going to make her happy and take care of her."*

Fletcher walks up to him and says with a smile, *"We will see about that, but let's just start with today."* He embraced his soon-to-be son-in-law and told him he loved him. *"I have no doubt that my Pudding is loved."*

Karson dapped him up and said, *"Man, I'm so glad I have a brother."*

Jonathan felt less stressed and visibly relaxed. You could see a sense of calm come over him. It was time to go to get his bride.

Although it was July, the day was breezy and slightly overcast. Karrington held onto her dad's arm as if he was a toddler learning to walk again. He looked at her and said, *"Pudding, I love you. You will be a great wife, but know your daddy is always here."*

Fletcher is a man of few words but when he spoke, his words were impactful and heartfelt. Karrington knew what her dad meant. They had their own language. Just as a tear dropped from her eye the doors opened and her dad led her down the aisle.

Karrington's beauty was undeniable. Her dark reddish hair was pulled up in a bun. Her simple, satin sweetheart-neckline dress laid on her body like a second skin. Her only accessory was a strand of choker pearls that her mother had lent her. She looked like a princess. When she was almost within arm's reach of Jonathan, she could see that he was very emotional and in that moment all of her doubts melted away.

The wedding was beautiful and the guests danced until sunrise. The newlyweds left the following day for Fiji for five days. Once they returned from their honeymoon, Karrington and Jonathan returned to Morgantown. They packed up the rest of her things, and hit the road to start their new life together. Jonathan had to be at practice at the end of the month and Karrington's first class was also scheduled for the end of next month. They wanted to spend a minute being a married couple before these obligations started to demand their attention in earnest.

 For the next two weeks, the newlyweds fixed up their new apartment and got settled in. They went to Aspen for a second honeymoon where they attended some festivals, did some hiking, got massages, and continued to enjoy each other.
They went to Denver where Karrington would be going to school. They timed her commute from home to school. The 70-mile drive will be exactly what Karrington needed to decompress from her day before returning home to her husband. They were ready to live a life that would be perfect for them.

Law School

OLYMPICS, AND MARRIED LIFE...

Karrington and Jonathan were married a month after her graduation because they didn't want to wait until Jonathan returned from Olympic camp. He will be in practice for at least four years and Karrington will be in law school for at least three years. Karrington and Jonathan had mutual respect. They are both Virgos so time and space are their magical powers. They never smother each other. They could be away from each other without worrying about what the other is doing or being jealous. They respect each other's space. Their admiration for each other was undeniable.

Jonathan followed a strict diet. For breakfast, he eats four egg whites with water. Lunch is a salad with protein, and dinner is vegetables. Truth is, Karrington didn't mind his strict diet because it helped her too. She was fine as long as she could have some ice cream from time to time. Jonathon enters their apartment to see Karrington who makes it home before him every day. *"Hey, babe. How was your day?"*

She quickly jumped off the couch to greet him with a hug and kiss. *"It's so much better now that you are here. I'm so glad you are home!"*

Jonathan picked her up and carried her into their bedroom. He drops her on their bed and starts to remove his clothing. Looking intently at him, she began to remove her clothes and he mirrors her actions. When they were both naked, he picked her up again and carried her into the shower. It's like they had a telepathic code because they were no longer using their words. He was still carrying her as she turned on the water.

He steps into the shower and slowly lets her down as the water begins to cover her hair and face. Jonathan's managed to memorize his wife's body so well that he could navigate without having to interrupt their kisses. His hands move lower and lower until he finally hears her gasp. He continues to tease her with his fingers until her pleasure bud is swollen and she is ready to release for him. He commands her to wait, as he picks up her limp body and positions her on top of his manhood. Moans and groans were all they released. Most of their days followed this pattern with scheduled rest periods that they had agreed on.

Days turned into weeks, weeks turned into months, and months into years. Jonathan's training became more rigorous and law school, more demanding. Something that would easily break other couples made Jonathan and Karrington stronger. They motivated each other and gave each other space when needed. When one spouse was in need, the other would be right there.

Karrington was finishing up law school and preparing for graduation. Meanwhile, Jonathan was on his way to fulfilling his other lifelong dream. They were living the lives they wanted for each other and they were happy. Karrington started preparing for her family friends and in-laws coming for her graduation.

Karrington was ecstatic to see Gabby, Lillian, and Morgan. They hadn't seen each other since Lillian's wedding over a year prior. Karrington wanted the girls to get there early so they could have some girls' time before everyone made it in. They talked about school, marriage, and how they missed the simple days. Karrington let them know that things had been going well with her and Jonathan and what was next for her. She had a position in the law office in town just some low-level work, but she was grateful to be in the mix. Tomorrow was graduation and she was so excited for her and Jonathan. All their dreams were coming true.

After graduation, Karrington and Jonathan celebrated with their families. But eventually, everyone went home and they got back to their regular schedule. Karrington was getting settled in her new office, and Jonathan was going through his medical training so he could progress to the next level. He had been working and training hard. This was fine, because Karrington had work in the evenings, but his training had increased.

Karrington and Jonathan had a very strong connection and understanding. Their communication was impeccable and clear there were never any misunderstandings even when they disagreed. They were able to talk about it without ever being disrespectful to each other. Although their careers were pulling and pushing them in different directions, they always ate together, loved each other, and had date nights once a week. They were happy and had their entire life to enjoy each other. They were even ready to start a family. Jonathan had two months until he had concrete information about the Olympics and he would be one of the top runners for the United States of America.

Karrington and Jonathan were on their way to having a great life. She had just won her first case and Jonathan had to go in for his physical consultation, the final hurdle for all of his hard work. The Olympic training was starting at the top of the week. When he went in on Monday, he called Karrington to let her know he wanted to celebrate tonight.

Jonathan was so happy and proud of his wife. Karrington had been exceptional since the day he met her and she had never disappointed him. *"Pretty girl, I'm on my way to the consultation. Meet me in our spot and wear something nice. I have a wonderful evening planned for us tonight!"*

Karrington was driving home but she could hear his voice coming through her speakers and she could hear how proud he was of himself. *"Baby, what time do you want me to be there,"* she asked.

He replied, *"An hour. I'll have a car to pick you up and I will meet you at our special place."*

Jonathan hung up with Karrington as he pulled into he facility. When Jonathan checked in, he saw his coach. That was a surprise because he wasn't expecting him to be there. *"Jake, what are you doing here? Do you have a meeting tonight?"*

Jake Lewis was always jovial but firm, but this time was different. Jonathan could only describe his expression as troubling. *"Jon, we need to talk to you."*

Jonathan went into the conference room with no problem. He had never done this before. Maybe this was something else he had to do to qualify for the Olympics. *"Jon, we are here to let you know something. There is no easy way to say this, but you will not be able to qualify for the Olympics due to your physical results."*

Jonathan was confused. The coaches continued to explain that sadly, his plan to go to the Olympics had come to an end. Jonathan was stunned. He was informed of the next steps then he left to meet his wife who was waiting for him.

On Jonathan's drive to the restaurant, he didn't know how he was going to tell Karrington that what he had worked so hard for was over. They had always been so honest with each other — no need to change it now. He pulled up to the valet and got out in search of his wife. Karrington was there just as he had expected and just as beautiful as he knew she would be. Jonathan walked over to her and kissed her on the cheek. She knew something was wrong before he was through kissing her.

"Baby, what's wrong? Do we need to leave? You don't look like we need to be here." Jonathan was silent so she continued, "Baby, what is the problem? Talk to me."

This is what he loved about his wife. She always knew everything about him instinctively. He didn't know how she knew. Maybe it was the lawyer in her but he loved her so much for it. Karrington always knew how to make him feel like it was always just the two of them even in the middle of a crowd. Jonathan opted for them to leave the restaurant.

Karrington knew that something was truly wrong because he wanted to go to In-N-Out Burger. She looked at him and said, *"In and Out burger? Baby, this is not your usual meal."*

Still, Jonathan was quiet. They ordered their meal and they drove home.

They made it home. Karrington undressed and put on one of his T-shirts while he walked, seemingly in a trance, and then he sat on the couch. Karrington sat next to him, and said, *"Baby, talk to me."* Her tone was soft and calming, as she took his hand.

Jonathan slid his arm around her waist and pulled her close. She could see immense sadness in his eyes, but she was intentionally quiet and waited for her husband to speak. *"Baby, I have done everything right. But when I went for my physical, they did a muscle check and found that I have stress fractures in my legs."*

Karrington only just nodded and he continued, *"I will have to be in a brace for 6 to 8 weeks and the final trials for the Olympics ended today. I can't start on Monday."* Karrington did not know what to say she moved in closer and held her husband. They sat there for what felt like forever. They talked about what was next, knowing they could get through the crisis, no matter what. Their trajectory for their life hit a hurdle but they had each other. There was nothing they could not do or get through together.

Nothing could have prepared Karrington for what came next.

3

Months Later...

Karrington poured herself into her work. It had become a struggle for her to be successful while her husband was in such a dark place. Jonathan not being able to run was like Superman not being able to fly anymore. Karrington's workload had somehow become heavier as she was en route to becoming a top DA in her office. She sometimes felt guilty for celebrating her accomplishments while Jonathan was dealing with such a traumatic reality.

Jonathan was her best friend and they talked about everything, but she didn't feel as comfortable talking to him anymore. These days, Jonathan was so distant, and Karrington felt she couldn't talk to him. When Jonathan went to have his cast put on, he was told they were physical therapy and modified training he could possibly be ready for the Olympics in four years. It seemed he began to resent Karrington for achieving her dreams while he had to give up his. He became mean and detached, often refusing to speak to her.

Their sex life was nonexistent. When Karrington tried to touch him or kiss him, he would pull away. Many nights she would lay next to him naked and he would ask her to put something on before she got sick. He often made smart remarks about her profession. Karrington could hardly recognize her best friend and husband these days. The man she had loved for so long seemed to be slipping away.

Jonathan was in the kitchen, and dropped a glass on the floor. Karrington asked from the other room, *"Honey, are you ok?"*

He seemed to be aggravated by everything Karrington says or does and this moment was no different. *"Oh, don't sue me. I'm sorry if I broke a glass."*

That was it. Her heart broke in that moment and she recalled what her father had said before walking her down the aisle, that she can always come back home. She wished that she was at home. She had never felt more alone than she did at that moment. Jonathan was no longer the person that she had known for the past eight years. This man in her home was foreign to her. She tried so hard to make him happy, to minimize herself, and try to stay out of his way. Deep down inside she knew that this was not love. The saddest part was that she didn't know how she would get it back or if she even wanted to try to get it back.

Karrington's girls were all busy with their lives. Their only connection was their group chat. The only place she could turn was to the group chat with her friends. She needed them like never before.

She called Gabby to tell her what was going on. Gabby booked the first flight out before Karrington even finished speaking. She would arrive the next day. That was perfect because Jonathan would be going to Sikeston, Missouri to visit his mom for the weekend. He told Karrington that he would be more needed and useful there.

When Karrington hung up with Gabby, she called her dad to fill him in on everything that was happening. Fletcher was ready to come to Colorado to see his Pudding. He called her every other day and on the days that he didn't call, he texted. She appreciated their conversations and how he tactfully updated her mom behind the scenes. Some calls included all three of them. Her parents' unwavering love and support made her feel like she could get through anything.

Gabby arrived the next day and helped Karrington so much! She just needed something familiar for a minute. Gabby left on the Sunday morning before Jonathan returned that night. When he got home, he looked different to her, and not in a good way. He greeted her with a hug and kiss and told her they needed to talk.

She was always so enthralled when he spoke. She believed in him still even if he didn't believe in himself. Even though Karrington was hurt by everything that had happened since his injury, she couldn't help being glad to see him. She sat up on the couch and became very attentive, *"Baby, what is it?"*

"Baby, I know this may not be what we need to do, but while I was home I ran into one of my friends from high school. He is a coach at my old high school and the school is in need of a track and field coach. I know I should have called you and talked it over with you, but I went to the interview and I got the job!"

Karrington did not know how to feel or what to say. On one hand, the man standing in front of her was the one she had been missing for the last three months. On the other hand, the problem would be moving to Sikeston and giving up the life and career that she has built in Colorado for him.

AND HEARTBREAK...

Karrington was very loyal and in her mind, she belonged with her husband. So, she had to compromise once again for him. She put in her notice at the firm and helped the colleague who would be taking her position. Karrington never saw a move to Sikeston coming. But if this would get her husband back and their love back, she would do it.

Jonathan hadn't been this excited in a while. Her marriage was the most important thing to her and when he kissed her, she felt compromising was the right thing to do. She felt she was getting her husband back. Yet, she just couldn't help but think about how she had felt when she had to give up her preferred law school for him. Once again, it felt like she was the one giving up on a dream and making a sacrifice for the union.

Karrington began looking for jobs in Missouri and Jonathan seemed to feel better with every passing day. All the while, she was becoming annoyed because for the first time, Jonathan hadn't checked on her. It seemed as if he didn't realize or care what she was giving up for him. It seemed like he didn't care how hard she had worked here in Colorado to become a top DA, or that her needs were not being met. Not once did Jonathan acknowledge that she was giving everything up for him, again. She said goodbye to her firm and in the next two days they were on the road to Missouri.

Jonathan and Karrington made it to Missouri. For the time being, they would be living with his family until the high school opened in Fall. Karrington found a small firm where she had to start over at a lower level. This was the first time since graduation that she felt as if she was a target like when she was home in Morgantown. She could sense the negative whispers that strangers made about her. She knew people were second-guessing her point of view, and she noticed that she did not get certain cases that she could do with her eyes closed.

Through all of it, she tried to prioritize her husband and his happiness, but she was fast becoming uneasy and unhappy. Karrington tried to settle in but there were so many factors. On top of the awkwardness and discomfort at work, she had to get used to not having her own space at "home". Date nights with Jonathan went from being four nights a month at five-star spots to impromptu trips to the local steakhouse whenever his mom didn't cook.
This was far from what Karrington had envisioned for her life!

Jonathan was happy. The school year was in full swing and he was connected to anything and everything associated with track and field. He started going out more with coworkers after practice so Karrington was forced to spend most of her nights with his mom instead of with her husband. She also noticed that he was on his phone more than usual. It seemed like he was settling in well, but not her. Jonathan no longer spoke about the Olympics or his physical therapy. Karrington observed that he was not as active as he used to be, even as a coach. Surely, she did not give up everything and move across the country for him to let himself go and demote her as a priority. Resentment was building within her and she was struggling.

As this track and field season ended, Karrington came to the end of her rope. She and Jonathan had been in counseling and he had completely stopped being intimate with her. Karrington has her suspicions, that's the lawyer in her, but the love she was trying to hold onto doesn't let her go all the way there. Whenever she mentions them moving into their own place, he would get angry and start a fight for no apparent reason. Karrington was so unhappy and she felt stuck in this five-signal light town. She felt so alone. She needed her family, so she reached out to her mother.

Karrington called her mom and confided in her. Katherine always was a shield for her children. You could hear her take a deep breath before she started to respond to Karrington, trying to hold her tears back. Kathrine's heart was breaking for her daughter. She finally spoke.

"I would never tell you to leave your husband, baby. But what I will tell you is to make sure you are happy. You are in control of your own happiness. I love you and I am right here."

Karrington knew what that meant.

When Katherine hung up the phone she began to weep. She went to the bathroom to clean up her face before walking into the room where Fletcher was. *"Your Pudding is coming home,"* was all she said.

Fletcher immediately picked his phone up and found one of those fancy apps Katherine had added to his phone and sent his Pudding $5000. He followed that up with a text that simply said, *"You know your daddy is always here. See you soon."*

When Karrington hung up the phone, she knew that she was going to hear from her daddy. As soon as she heard her money app beep and she saw the familiar words that her dad had said to her on her wedding day, her decision became clear. There was nothing left for her to do but pack up and go home.

Karrington started making moves for her happiness. The counseling wasn't working, Jonathan didn't respond to her anymore, and she was alone. She took a couple of days off from her job to begin her process of getting back to herself.

Karrington began to look for a new job closer to home. She found a thriving DA's office in Fairmont. She told Jonathan she was going to homecoming to see the girls but Karrington never went to Huntsville. Instead, she went to Fairmont to interview with a DA's office and she got the job! She knew she would; her references were amazing and she was an exceptional attorney. She didn't need a reference from her current employment because Colorado was impressive enough.

McCullin & Lewis was a thriving company led by the no-nonsense top DA of Fairmont, WV and she was told that she would meet him once she started the job. Karrington went back to Sikeston and told Jonathan what she was planning to do. To her surprise, he didn't put up a fight and for the first time in a long time, Karrington could exhale.

Jonathan told her that he knew that she did not go to homecoming and stated that was his reason for deciding to move on with his life. He told her that he had no place in his life for a liar. He then revealed that he had been seeing a woman who was able to understand where he was coming from and where he is trying to go. A woman who could respect him and love him for the man he is.

Karrington remained quiet and turned her back to Jonathan as reality hit. Suddenly, her eyes roamed the living room and she noticed for the first time that her things had been packed into boxes. With a deep breath, she fought back tears and ran through a mental list of her belongings as she checked the boxes. Realizing that a couple of her things were missing, Karrington walked off toward the bedroom. The faint sound of water running in the bathroom was drowned out by the sound of her breaking heart. She noticed an unfamiliar handbag bag on the bed. As she stood there puzzled, a woman walked out of the bathroom wrapped in a towel.

Karrington gasped as she recognized the woman as an employee at the nearby grocery store. *You've got to be fucking kidding me,* she thought. Jonathan had moved the grocery store lady into his mom's house. The lady looked at her as if she was an unwanted, soiled dish towel. Karrington had never felt so disrespected in her life. She never thought in a million years that Jonathan would do something so callous and heartless. While Miss Grocery

Store continued to stare at her, Karrington gathered the rest of her belongings and walked out of the bedroom without a word.

Jonathan's mother had come to resent Karrington and felt as if she was not supportive of her son. She told Karrington plainly to leave her house.

Karrington never raised her voice. Her heart was shattered. She had wrongfully thought that she could have talked this out with Jonathan because they had loved each other in their marriage. She could not believe that he would do her like this. Karrington only had the money that her father had sent her. Luckily, it was enough for her to leave immediately and get a hotel for the night.

Further investigation confirmed that Jonathan had met Miss Grocery Store when he applied for the coach position and had been in constant contact with her since then. This explains why he was uninterested in being intimate with his wife and had checked out of his marriage. Karrington was devastated.

Karrington cried all night in the hotel bed. As the night went on, she went from being sad to furious. She thought about everything she had given up for Jonathan. She dried her eyes, took a shower, and went to bed with a new mindset. *Karrington, you will be fine. This was supposed to happen.*

She fell asleep soon afterwards and for the first time in a long time, slept peacefully. The next morning she got up, packed her car, and headed home to West Virginia. She called her family and her friends and she told them what had transpired. She made sure to state that she was OK and that she would be home soon. Although she was still a little heartbroken and in shock, she knew that somehow this was a blessing in disguise. She looked forward to new beginnings.

Happiness is
ON THE WAY...

Karrington made it back home to West Virginia and opted to stay with her parents until she was able to secure her own space. She needed to be home for a while. She needed to feel love. It had been a long time since she'd been in its presence. Within a week she was getting settled into her new condo, her new office, and her new life. Her girlfriends came to visit her. She knew she could always depend on them. They helped to make her new transition smooth and effortless.

She told them about her new job and her new superior co-worker. As they were sitting and catching up, Karrington was happy and she was feeling like herself again. Gabby asked her about her office environment.

Karrington was more than happy to talk about the only environment she was quietly using in her head to get back to herself. *"Girl, let me tell you. The Senior DA is the sexiest man alive. His name is Dominique McCullin, but I haven't met him yet. I was told I will meet him when I finish with the initial welcome program and paperwork,"* she told Gabby with a big smile on her face.

Gabby laughed. *"Please don't go out here with your inner hoe tendencies and get fired before you start! I asked about the environment, not what you want to get under to get over!"*

The girls all laughed and Karrington continued, *"Tomorrow is my first day and it has to be a great firm. The person who interviewed me is top tier and he is nowhere near Dominique's status."*

Then Gabby said with a voice of concern, *"Real talk, Karri. Take your time and heal. That's the best thing you can do for yourself right now."*

Karrington knew her friend was right. The girls continued to enjoy each other before everyone left the next morning. They elebrated her move and her divorce being finalized.

Monday morning came quick and Karrington was excited and nervous at the same time. She had laid her clothes out the night before like it was her first day of high school. When she made it to her new office, she was given a case to look over as well as the remainder of her preliminary initial hire work. She loved the firm already because her opinion was valued. They wanted to know what were her thoughts on a case by the end of the week.

Karrington knew this was a test to see if she was worth the hype, which she was. This was what she loved about being an attorney — the challenge. This was also different and welcomed. It was the opposite of her previous job in Sikeston. This firm seemed to care about what she had to offer. As the week progressed, she caught glimpses of her senior exec crush and put a plan in place to introduce herself.

Karrington was a formidable lawyer who was up for any and all challenges. *Looks like I have to take this into my own hands. Mr. McCullin leaves at 5:00 every day. So, maybe I could just make sure I bump into him on my way out.* Karrington began to laugh at herself as she continued her paperwork and finished looking through her case.

Karrington had started packing her things to leave. She had turned around to reach for something on her back table when she heard a deep voice say, *"Hello. You're the new kid on the block. Karrington, right?"*

When she slowly turned around, she instantly knew. She gasped and let out a whisper, *"Dominque."*

The petals of the rose are
the most important

It's ya girl Millichun!!!
Follow me to find out
@millichun